Walt Disney's
AMERICAN CLASSICS
Pecos Bill

Starlight Editions

Twin Books

Pecos Bill was known as the roughest, toughest cowboy in Texas history. Tall tales just naturally grew up around him—like the one about how he got his name.

Bill was just a baby at the time. His ma and pa were heading West in a covered wagon with his fifteen brothers and sisters and a couple of hound dogs. Poor Bill fell out of the wagon when they crossed the Pecos River, and his folks didn't even miss him! And there he sat—homeless as a poker chip in the ruggedest land in the West. So that's why they call him "Pecos Bill."

Lucky for Bill, there was a coyote den nearby. He crawled in there and curled up with the pups. When Ma Coyote came home, she thought the stork had left her a surprise. But Bill looked so much at home that she took him in and raised him like one of her own.

Pretty soon, young Bill was top dog in that coyote pack. He laid claim to the biggest bones and the best of everything else—and nobody gave him a fight. He could yell so loud it would curl the hair on a bear. And he just plain had to be the best at whatever he tackled. Once he was boss of all the coyotes . . .

. . .Bill took on the rest of the local critters. He outloped the antelope, outjumped the jackrabbit, and even outhissed the rattlesnake! They didn't come any tougher than young Bill. And nobody knew the Pecos land like he did.

One scorching hot day, Bill climbed up to his favorite look-out and saw a colt in big trouble. The colt had the staggers from the heat, and the vultures were forming up a welcoming committee. Had to be fifty of them dive-bombing that poor little horse. Bill's fighting spirit was roused up, and he shinnied down that rock in a minute flat.

Biff! Bam! Bill punched his way into that cloud of vultures and black feathers started flying all over the place. A minute later, those mean old birds looked like a bunch of plucked chickens! Bill had them on the run, and that lost colt was mighty happy to see him.

When the feathers settled, young Bill and that colt laughed right out loud and took off across the desert at a run. "Widdermaker," Bill called the colt, and he was every bit as fearless as Bill himself. The two of 'em stuck together like warts on a toad from that day on.

As Bill got bigger, he set out to become the best cowboy in the West. He'd pick up a rattlesnake and make a lasso of him. Then he and Widdermaker would practice roping, running and riding bareback the livelong day. Not a critter would stand in their way when they lit out across Pecos country.

When Bill got older, he sometimes rode through town at a gallop, yelling "*Yahoo!*" and twirling his lasso just for fun. Folks scattered every which way when they heard him coming. No one knew what Pecos Bill would get up to next, but there were plenty of stories about his doings . . .

. . . like the time he roped a ragin' cyclone out of nowhere and rode it like a bucking bronco. No matter how hard that cyclone tried to throw him, Bill stuck like a burr. And Widdermaker dug in his hoofs like a real cow pony and held on tight. Between them, they tamed that ornery cyclone down to a little breeze!

Then there was the time when the Big Drought hit Texas. There was no rain for so long that folks forgot what water looked like. Bones were bleachin' in the desert.

Bill and Widdermaker lost their way one day, and the vultures started lookin' hopeful. Man and beast, they were almost goners when they reached a sign that read "No Water" any way you looked at it.

Bill got so mad that he forgot how low he'd been feelin'. He ripped that sign right out of the ground and used the post to dig the Rio Grande!

"Yippee-i-yay!" he yelled, riding along the river twirling his six-guns.

But all of a sudden, down the river came a sight that stopped Bill right in his tracks. It was the famous cowgirl Slewfoot Sue, riding a giant catfish! Sue sure could handle a rope, because that big old catfish was jumping right through her lasso.

Bill's heart started thumpin' like a cattle stampede. He was plumb fixed to the spot, and poor Widdermaker didn't know what to make of it all. Looked like trouble to him, and he sure was right.

Sue dismounted her catfish at the river's edge and took to arranging her hair as if she hardly noticed Bill at all. He was so tongue-tied shy that he opened his mouth to say hello and nothing came out. But when he fumbled to tip his hat, Sue couldn't help noticing in her mirror.

"How do?" said Slewfoot Sue.

Well, Bill was set on getting that girl from the start, and before you knew it, they were engaged. Sue got herself a fancy dress with a bustle in the back. Bill picked a big bouquet, and the sheriff turned out to hear their vows. But one member of the wedding party was fit to be tied. That was Widdermaker; he was mighty jealous. He plain couldn't stand Sweet Sue, and she felt the same about him. So Sue started real trouble when she said to Bill, "I want to get married a-ridin' your horse."

It took four strong men to hold down Widdermaker when Sue mounted up for the wedding. That horse was seethin' inside, but Sue paid him no mind. She was out to prove she could tame both Pecos Bill *and* his horse. The whole town turned out to see what would happen.

Right then, Widdermaker tore loose of the cowpokes holding the ropes and leaped for the sky. He bucked, he pawed, he pranced, he danced. But Sue stuck like glue—until her bustle started to bounce. That steel-and-wire contraption worked just like a spring to send that gal higher and higher!

Sue was still gainin' altitude on every bounce when the reins snapped and she took off like a rocket. Far over the heads of the crowd she flew, and she kept on flyin' 'til she was just a little speck in the sky. All of a sudden, Sue dropped down to earth, but that troublesome bustle made her bounce back up again! Folks' jaws were droppin', but Bill stepped up with his trusty rope, ready to fetch her down. And he'd never been known to miss.

The crowd breathed a sigh as Bill made his loop with careless ease. Then he whirled it and twirled it and let it fly—but he never saw his horse's hoof come down on that rope and spoil his throw. Old Widdermaker just stared at the sky, real innocent-like.

The rope fell short, and Sue kept on going. On each bounce, she flew a bit higher. Poor Sue flew all the way to the moon, and there she's stayed to this very day.

Pecos Bill was so busted up that he almost went back to the coyote pack. But he never knew that his horse had come between him and his one true love. Sometimes, he still rides up to his favorite look-out to stare at the moon and sing a lonesome cowboy song. And if you listen real carefully, you can hear the coyotes howlin' right along with him.